HELLO COMPUTER

Drew D. Lenhart

Copyright © 2024 Drew D. Lenhart

All rights reserved. This book or any portion thereof may not be reproduced or used in any manner whatsoever without the express written permission of the publisher except for the use of brief quotations in a book review.

Originally published in 2019.

Printed in the United States of America

Cover design and logo by Drew D. Lenhart

Cover illustration by Mike Cody

I stared at our first electrical bill and couldn't move.

Down at the bottom, the last number listed by the word TOTAL. The number was high. Sky high. It was almost as much as our house payment.

Mom is going to lose it. We barely have any money left over after moving into the new house. This will probably mean extra shifts at the diner for Mom. In fact, it might mean extra shifts for me too. I was coming up on fifteen and working as a busboy at the local diner is not fun work at all.

I could not believe it, and I stared longer at the bill. Appreciating the power company's blue logo, I quickly went from liking it to wanting to curse out loud.

With trembling hands, I folded the bill, my eyes widening in disbelief at the staggering amount. I fought the urge to scream.

We've only lived in the house for a month and a half. There was no logical reason it could be this high. It has to be a fluke. Calling the power company did no good, as the lady on the phone insisted the bill was correct, looking up on her computer several times to verify. I even asked her to triple check for good measure.

She loudly tapped away on her keyboard. The punching sound of each keystroke echoed through the phone's speaker, agitating my ears. Somehow, we had churned through enough energy to power our home, plus two more!

How? We still have everything we own meticulously packed away in boxes and stacked in our living room. We have nothing plugged in yet except for the essentials.

Mom and I moved into this house with much eagerness. She saved every single penny she could for years, working double and sometimes triple shifts just to scrape enough money together for this house!

Apartment living had slowly eroded our faith in humanity. Home ownership was our only escape from the craziness that ensued at the apartment building: guns, violence and loud parties, just to name a few. It took us several years of saving. Close to eight years, but we made it to homeownership. We were finally free.

Finding our new house couldn't have come at a better time, as Mom finally snapped. It was the constant noise abuse from the neighbor above us. I had always known it was only a matter of time.

* * * *

The new house had been our home for two and a half months now. We had unpacked every single box, making the house livable to some sort of standard.

I stood on the porch in the 110° heat and chuckled.

After growing up in southern Texas, I was used to the heat. This was nothing. Totally normal. Living in the great state of Texas had conditioned me, prepared me. It also contributed to my year-round tanned skin and dirty blonde hair. I'm not sure if the Texas heat gave me my height, but I was becoming super tall for my age, nearing six feet.

I opened the metal flap to our black stainless-steel mailbox mounted to the house, admiring my somewhat limited do-it-yourself skills. A new mailbox was my first project. I was proud of the effort.

I grabbed the day's mail and noticed the blue logo of the power company in the top left corner. My heart sank a little, instantly remembering how painful it was for Mom to pay off the last one. I opened it immediately, letting the envelope float slowly to the ground.

Once again, the bill was exorbitant, too high. I wadded the bill into a ball and threw it against the wall in anger. I walked inside and let the screen door slam against the doorjamb.

* * * *

Three and a half months now at the new house, I'm again staring down at the latest electricity bill. I managed to grab the bill before Mom had the chance to stress over it.

Somehow, it's higher than the previous month! Mom stepped out onto the porch while I stared down at the bill. She stood next to me in her blue tank top and shorts, almost afraid to come outside, afraid that the sun would burn her fair skin.

"Darren, why don't we call the power company or an electrician? They can come out with their little tester things and find out what the problem is," suggested Mom, acting like the know-it-all of electricity.

"Tester things?" I questioned. "I suppose they could come out and at least do something or give some kind of advice."

I wouldn't know. I wasn't anywhere near an expert of any kind.

"Perfect, I'll see if we can get someone out here as soon as possible!" said Mom.

The electrician packed up his testing equipment and carefully wrapped the wiring of the testing prongs around his tinged yellow voltmeter.

"I don't know what to tell you," said the electrician. "I've checked every outlet. Checked each of the big appliances with a watt usage monitor. I've even ensured that the electrical box is up to date. Everything looks perfect!"

"How about the electrical work? Come on, there has to be something," I complained, all the while leaning against a wall with both of my hands in my pockets.

"All the wiring in the house is up to code. All the wiring in the house meets the latest code requirements. Heck, almost everything is brand new! There is nothing in this house that is drawing that much power to cause your bill to skyrocket," he said.

I looked down at my feet. "There has to be something, some direction to take."

"I have a theory and an idea of what I think you should try next."

I looked up at the electrician with one last glimmer of hope, thinking of the last dreadful option: we may have to move out or, worse yet, go back to apartment living. I dreaded the thought.

"You should have the utility company come out and mark where underground electrical lines. Have them check all over your property. Sometimes people steal!!" he said.

"Steal what? Electricity?" I asked.

"Yep, I've seen this before. For instance, I've seen people run electrical lines over to a neighbor's outbuilding and siphon off their power. It's pretty rare, but it happens from time-to-time. How long have you lived here?" he asked.

"Almost four months," I answered.

"It's possible. The previous owners might have had deals with neighbors that you're unaware of. If I were you, I'd start there next!"

* * * *

The utility company finally came around after three more weeks and receiving another devastating electric bill. The representative was a tall, overweight man with large a handlebar mustache and greasy, long hair. He wore his bright neon yellow utility jacket while he held his utility device with both hands.

I met him on the front lawn and he barely acknowledged my existence. Apparently, I was a ghost. I don't mind as long as he finds something. I stood by, watching as he swayed his device back and forth. It was a device the size of a baseball bat, a computer screen at the top handle, and a sensor at the other end. As it beeped along, he pressed a button on his device and it sprayed red paint out of the bottom. The indication of the red color meant that there was an electrical line hidden below. He continued to sway the device back and forth, all the while spraying red paint up to the house.

He looked over at me as he approached the side of the house. "Must be your main feed. Ain't nothing else coming in here in the front. I'll do the back really quick and be on my way," he muttered.

I followed along, as he continued swaying the device, until we reached the backyard—our disgusting backyard. Our property butts up to the woods at the back. The home to the left is a vacant home, long ago abandoned by its owners. To the right of us, an old woman lives there whom we've barely seen. Luckily, both properties have a privacy fence. Combined with the woods and the fences, the backyard provides great privacy for us. Mom has dreamt of the possibilities from the first moment we saw the backyard.

The yard was burnt to a crisp from the summer heat. With drought and water restrictions placed on watering lawns occurring so frequently and pretty much all summer, the lawn suffered.

As I was looking at the burnt grass in disgust, the device beeped. The utility man had found something in the middle of the backyard and began marking the location. He sprayed four lines in the direction of the woods before the beeping stopped. "Stops here in the middle of your yard. Let's check and see if this line leads to your house."

He guessed correctly and marked a straight red dotted line leading to the outside electrical meter. A thought screamed at me in the back of my mind. Builders constructed the house in the mid-twentieth century during an era of much fear. I was about to blurt out what the mystery could be, but the utility man yelled, "I bet you there is an old bomb shelter buried in your yard!"

"That sure does make sense, but not why there is power down there. Why did the problem just start now? We received an average electric bill from the previous owner and nothing too crazy high," I responded.

"Who knows? Did you flip on any breakers when you moved in?" asked the utility man, standing with his meter thrown over his right shoulder.

The thought of *move in* day popped into my head. That day was a day hotter than normal with blistering weather, a super hot day even to my standards. It was so hot it looked like the house could melt away while we moved our belongings out of the moving truck.

He was right!

The house was vacant for several months, and the realtor explained the house was without power before handing over the keys to us. On the first day when we moved in, I flipped on every single breaker I saw in the basement!

"I think you need to get someone in here and dig this up, find out what's running in there," the utility man said, stating the obvious.

* * * *

Robert, my neighbor, lives across the street and owns a lawn service with all kinds of equipment he's purchased over the years. He is a chipper old man with balding, grey hair, in his mid fifties perhaps.

He's a friendly guy, always willing to help. He even tried helping us move in that fateful hot move-in day.

While patiently waiting for Robert to get his

mail one afternoon, I waited until he limped to his mailbox, knowing I'd have enough time to catch his attention. I always wondered if he had an interesting story behind his limp, perhaps an old interesting war story. I was too afraid to ask.

I ran outside, pretending as if I were doing something in the yard, and struck up a conversation. I tried to explain the situation.

Robert listened quietly while he held his mail. Looking as if he were eager to open them like an impatient child. I rambled on every detail I could think of while he listened. I explained I would like to uncover or at least find the entrance to the shelter.

Robert agreed and looked immensely intrigued by himself. He relayed he could help over the weekend so as not to interfere with his business work and would be happy to come over with his excavator, all for a free dinner at Mom's diner.

I agreed on her behalf, thinking she

wouldn't mind.

Mom and I enjoyed the bright Saturday morning. Well, Mom did anyway.

It was almost too bright as we ate our breakfast in the sunroom off the back of the house. The sun did everything it could do to bounce off every bright and reflective surface in sight, including my plate. I had to close my eyes as I shoveled scrambled eggs into my mouth.

Our peaceful morning soon turned into a loud rumbling noise. I looked up at Mom and saw just past her in the distance, Robert driving his small excavator into our backyard. The diesel engine's exhaust roared loudly and swirled around the side of the house. It filtered into the sunroom's screen windows, unsettling our peaceful morning with the smell of diesel and noise.

Mom turned up her nose as she ate her breakfast and breathed in the engine exhaust.

The little boy in me rushed to finish what I

was doing and ran inside to put on some clothes. I could feel Mom's disapproving stare drilling into the back of my head.

By the time I reached the backyard, Robert had already excavated most of it without me. I was so disappointed. Robert had large mounds of dirt already piled up at the edges. Inside the hole, the shelter looked like a concrete box! Dirt still lay on the box as Robert did the best he could with the bucket of the excavator.

He was able to find all the edges, which went down about five feet. The side closest to the house had a cylinder shaft higher than the concrete container with a door hatch on top of it.

I felt a little stupid, as the hatch would only have been a few inches under the soil. A simple metal detector and shovel probably could have discovered the door.

The rumble of the diesel engine quit, and Robert looked down at the shelter. "There she is. It's a bomb shelter alright."

"The hatch door. How in the heck am I going to get that open?" I said, inspecting the rusty edges of the door. Looking at it made me feel like I could contract tetanus.

"Easy! Use a hammer to move the handle in the open position, and then hook up a chain to the excavator and pull it open!" explained Robert.

He was right. It was easy, or Robert made it look easy. In no time at all, he pounded the rusted hatch handle into the open position and was pulling the door open with the excavator. The hatch screeched open, possibly waking the neighborhood.

As I peered into the entrance, Robert hobbled over to join me. We looked into the uncovered shelter together. A metal ladder, covered with rust, dust, and dirt, led all the way to the bottom from the inside.

"Robert, you've lived across the street from here for years, correct? None of the previous owners mentioned something like this?" I questioned, looking over at Robert.

"I briefly met the man and his wife. He was some sort of college professor. They both kept to themselves. Friendly, though, he always waved to me but never said much more than hello," replied Robert.

I focused on the entrance shaft, trying to count the number of steps on the ladder.

"Sorry I can't stay longer, Darren, but I have an appointment I need to get ready for. Tell me what you and your mom find down there? Also, tell your mother, don't forget about my free dinner!" said Robert, smiling as he returned to the excavator.

I nodded as I continued peering into the entrance. The possibility of this becoming an obsession concerned me, given my eagerness to uncover the truth behind the mystery.

What was down there? Would I simply find a room with old degrading survival supplies? It could be empty, or maybe there is something more. Thoughts of previous owners storing their valuables and finding those treasures intrigued me. Every time I thought about the bunker, I couldn't stop thinking about the possibilities.

It was time to get dirty and find the reality.

* * * *

My foot disturbed about a half inch of dust, which had been resting peacefully on the rusty metal ladder. I felt like I was disturbing sacred ground.

I used my foot to kick off the layer of dust before placing the middle of my foot firmly onto the step. I repeated the process on the next step and continued on until I reached the bottom of the floor.

At the base of the ladder, the years of dirt falling through the hatch crack became compressed underneath my footsteps. I clicked the flashlight on and looked around. The room was small and square-shaped, about 4 feet by 4 feet. I noticed a mounted rusty cylinder-shaped unit on the wall, about the size of a garbage can, with a pipe leading into the room and the other end leading up towards the hatch entrance. As I looked closer, on a fading manufacturer label, I could barely make out the text 'Carbon Dioxide Scrubber'.

My eye caught a second pipe leading out of the bunker, next to the CO2 scrubber pipe. I followed it with the flashlight as it twisted around each corner of the room down to the bottom corner of the small entryway. I didn't notice it at first, as it was rather small. A gas generator sat perfectly tucked into the corner with the pipe connected to its exhaust output. Smart! It looked brand new, preserved by the sealed environment of the bunker.

I inspected the generator, noticing it looked like nothing more than an old style internal combustion lawnmower engine, mounted on a piped reinforced cage for easy transportation. I noticed the engine had a rather large gasoline tank, which was probably intended so the owner wouldn't have to refuel as often.

Behind me, there was a small opening in a gray metal door. I found myself in the bomb shelter's entryway! My mind seemed to accept this was normal for bomb shelters, even though I had no working knowledge of them.

I used the flashlight to inspect the door. It was as normal as any other metal door. Untouched by weather and age, it looked brand new with a shiny silver handle. Shifting the flashlight to my right hand, I grabbed the handle and pulled it open. The door screeched as its metal rubbed against the doorjamb, causing my head to sink in agony. Almost instantly, hot air rushed out of the room as if a heater had just kicked on. Immediately, my eyes started to dry out, and I blinked several times to regain clarity.

The room brimmed with darkness, except for several small red and green blinking lights, all flashing this way and that in different and seemingly random patterns. The hot air dissipated from the room and normalized to the outside temperature.

I stepped inside, shining the flashlight in front of me. I bounced the light back and forth to get the lay of the room. It was quite large, roughly 12' by 12'. The sound of several large machines hummed on both sides of the small space. The reflection of the flashlight shone off of what looked like a computer monitor sitting at the far end of the room. Two lights hung from the ceiling, with the beam of the flashlight bouncing off their rims. I looked around for the switch.

As with any typical room, the switch was located by the door. I pulled the switch up, and it resisted, much like everything else here. It didn't give into change but I forced it into the up position. With a mix of fresh energy, the switch snapped loudly and popped, illuminating the room.

The room was incredible. I was expecting a

shelter: food, beds, and endless supplies. But none of the things you would typically find in a bomb shelter were present. What I was standing in seemed like a data center. An old data center from the past, complete with raised flooring and a room so loud with computer equipment, you couldn't think.

To my left and right, the large black mainframes hummed. Beside me, two units stood taller than me. The branding showed ST/400 on each unit in the upper left-hand corner. The logo was red and indented and each unit had four rows of its own, which looked like rows and rows of logic boards with their blinking lights shining through the plastic protective door cover.

I've seen pictures of these mainframes in images on the internet, but I've never seen one up close. I even remember using the pictures of these exact machines in an old middle school report about vintage computers!

Being a bit of a computer nerd myself, I've

never really seen the inside of a room like this. Modern data centers these days are much more efficient than the time era this equipment is from. We no longer needed giant buildings housing endless rows of computer servers to serve the world's internet and computing needs; instead, modular data centers orbit the Earth.

My eyes locked onto the terminal at the end of the room. A beige computer monitor. I walked past the mainframes closer to the terminal, leaving footprints on the dirty floor. I guessed that nobody had occupied this room in thirty or more years. Further, just past the mainframes, there stood smaller half size mainframe units with large spinning circles. Tape drives perhaps, spinning to the exact location that the computer is seeking.

There were four units total, lined up nicely against the concrete wall. I assumed it was a storage array. The spinning wheels were spinning extremely fast for several seconds in a random pattern. They stopped and paused before picking back up again. Perhaps there was some program running on the mainframe needing data?

I sat down on the stool before the terminal, wiping away excess dust before sitting. I clapped my hands together, letting the dust float to the ground.

A green line blinked on the lower left hand of the monitor. I supposed it was waiting for a command. I pounded the space bar several times. The cylinder tape drives to my left immediately spun and buzzed from the interaction.

The mainframes came alive behind me with what sounded like a rush of a thousand fans synchronously starting and stopping at the same time.

The screen began to show green text, appearing slowly and one letter at a time. "Hello, would you like voice interaction? (YES/NO)"

I looked at the keyboard for the keys and typed 'YES' with my index finger. The keys looked dingy from use and the plastic looked like a murky yellow, showing its age.

The cylinder drives buzzed again, and a synthesized voice cracked over loudspeakers. I jumped up, startled by the crackling noise, and noticed large speakers in the upper corners of the room. The noise sounded as if the computer were trying to adjust the sound volume as the speakers cracked and popped for several more seconds.

The synthesized voice began speaking as text slowly appeared on the screen. "Hello, system diagnostics indicate that battery supply is no longer sufficient. Please enter the current date, followed by current time, into the system."

Looking down, I looked for the number row and punched in 08-20-2029 11:00AM and pressed enter.

The computer buzzed for a few seconds

before returning the blinking green line. "Would you like to replay the last calculated scenario?" asked the mainframe.

Curiously, I typed 'YES' followed by the enter key. Nothing happened. I waited a few seconds before re-typing the command.

New text appeared on the screen as the mainframe instructed, "Press the talk button on the microphone or exit the program and answer NO on the voice prompt."

Next to the monitor stood a microphone. It was old and showing its rust. Below the microphone at the base, a faded green button. On the dingy button was a label and what looked like "TALK" written with a ballpoint pen.

"Would you like to replay the last calculated scenario?" questioned the mainframe.

I pushed the green talk button, unsure if the command would work. "Yes," I said.

The cylinder tape drives to my left instantaneously spun trying to retrieve records.

It seemed as if this would be a normal occurrence. I noted all the sounds of the moving pieces of the system and it was quite incredible.

Trying to get past all the noises, I reminded myself that the technology was old and unlike the computers of today.

"What is your name? Your speech patterns do not match the data stored in my database," questioned the computer.

"Darren," I said, holding the button.

"Thank you. Based on the latest trending data, unless all human pollution activity ceases to end by 2060, the atmosphere will no longer be able to harbor life."

"I would be able to provide a more accurate scenario by entering the latest data. Are you able to update data for the last 30 years?"

"No, I don't understand," I said, while holding the talk button. "What is this system used for? What is your purpose?"

"I was created by Professor Javier Holden

of the University of Southern Technology to store and model climate data at various designated areas around the world. These areas fed data into my system to model changes across the planet accurately and continually. My function is to create practical suggestions to resolve humanity's negative impact on the planet." Stated the mainframe.

"I still don't understand. When were you created? You are responding remarkably well to my speech." I asked, not believing the situation.

"As I stated, Javier Holden created me. My development was primarily conducted in the later 1980s with additional research teams contributing programming and hardware. Professor Holden developed my cognitive and speech engine. I officially came online in 1992."

"So, you are some form of artificial intelligence?" I asked.

"Yes, that is the best explanation."

I couldn't get over the idea of some kind of advanced artificial intelligence being created in that era of computing history. The responsiveness of the mainframe was superb and precise. I jokingly blurted out a joke to test the computer's abilities, "Can you tell me why the chicken crossed the road?"

I chuckled a little and waited for the computer's reply. The mainframes fan kicked on momentarily before the loudspeaker cracked on, "To get to the other side, of course. However, there are other logical reasons for the chicken to cross the road. Would you like to hear the top ten?"

"No, thanks." I said, disappointed, feeling outwitted by the computer.

This machine was incredible and was ahead of its time. Each time I pressed the button on the microphone, it translated my speech to text and I could hear the mainframe kick online, trying to process and understand the text. Incredible for technology nearing 40 years old. I asked the computer several more jokes out of curiosity if it could comprehend, as a test. If it did not know the answer, it asked me and stored the answer in its data bank.

"I appreciate all of your questions, but would you like me to finish replaying the last calculated scenario?" questioned the computer again.

"Yes, please do," I said, more convinced of the computer's validity. I was becoming more curious about the conclusions of the computer, and even more about the mysterious work of this Professor Holden.

"Considering the last dataset is from September 1999, we must assume that human activity and pollution have increased as the population increases, correct?" questioned the computer.

"Yes, yes, I would assume so." I stated, not giving the full extent of the last thirty years.

The computer was correct to assume so, as pollution has indeed increased. Air pollution is a dangerous problem for many cities and human health, massive deforestation, and reckless waste piling up in the oceans. The list goes on.

"I recommend we follow and execute the last plan."

"And what is that plan?" I asked, perking up.

"Professor Holden was able to tap into several nuclear power facilities across the world. After using all my system resources to gain access to these systems, we discovered massive security issues with these facilities. If those facilities are still online, I could initiate a system meltdown, causing multiple simultaneous nuclear explosions."

"Why would you do that? The damage would be far greater and millions of people would die!!" I said, practically yelling at the computer.

"Yes, precisely. Removing the human element out of the equation essentially stops the damage to the planet. The multiple explosions of the nuclear reactors would release enough dense smoke into the atmosphere to cool down the Earth for many, many years. This would give the planet ample time to repair itself."

I couldn't help but think perhaps there was a good reason this computer equipment was sitting in this bomb shelter. Professor Holden was planning to end the world in this very room.

"It is the best scenario with the best chances for Earth's survival. However, my communications device cannot communicate with the facilities. Do telephone lines still exist in 2029?" asked the computer.

A bad feeling hovered over me as every hair on my neck stood straight up and my hands turned ice cold. I felt I had stumbled into a dangerous area of a city, and I had the feeling of knowing something bad might happen to me If I stayed.

It felt wrong, almost treasonous having this conversation with the computer. Hacking nuclear power facilities? Professor Holden was smart enough to build this technology in a time where it was almost impossible. He built something incredible and was using it to destroy society. Is that what he really wanted?

"Darren, will you be able to help me with hooking up a telephone line?" asked the computer again.

"Yes, I think they still exist but," I paused, not knowing what to say. "I need to leave. It's getting late." I said, getting up to leave. Having heard all the information from the computer, that was the only response I could offer.

"Darren."

I climbed out of the room faster than I came down.

* * * *

Mom grilled me over dinner, asking me what was in the room. Recognizing her inevitable exploration, I made the decision to be truthful.

Well, almost all the truth. Describing all the equipment functioning and the old 1980s mainframe computer lining the sides of the room, I pointed out a single monitor sitting on a table at the end. I informed her that it might be broken because of its age and attempted to make it function, but couldn't get any display on the screen. Regrettably, I omitted the part about the plan to destroy the world. I told her when we moved in; we flipped on several of the unlabeled electrical breakers, and it caused our astronomical electric bills.

"So, are you going to power down the equipment?" asked Mom while she scooped a fork full of mashed potatoes.

"Yep. I'll power everything down. I'll find the breakers we originally turned on and make sure they stay off!"

"What are we going to do with it?" Mom asked.

"Not sure. I'll ask Robert if maybe he can

help me take it apart, recycle it or something. Maybe we can repurpose the room for its original function?" I suggested.

Mom laughed, "Yes, because this day and age we need to worry about nuclear war!"

I laughed, too. It was a silly notion, but after speaking to the computer, it didn't seem so silly.

Later, I relaxed on the couch and flipped the TV channel to the news. Sometimes, it bored me enough to put me to sleep. Perhaps it was a coincidence or fate was trying to tell me something. News cycle after news cycle reported issues around the world.

Half of the remaining Amazon rainforest is burning. The great plastic garbage patch in the Pacific Ocean is now the size of the United States. The President of the United States is considering a two-mile evacuation on the entire east coast of the United States in order to prepare for hurricane season. Last year's hurricane season was brutal and killed thousands. Pollution in China and India is so bad, they must stop their manufacturing several days a week to help with air quality.

I sat and thought about the computer in the bomb shelter. Could it be right about everything it said? If Professor Holden were alive today, what would he say, a giant 'I TOLD YOU SO'?

Much like the computer predicted, these issues happening in the world are because of humans!

I couldn't believe it. I was starting to justify the computer's outcomes. Destroy society so the Earth can have time to heal itself. Would it really be so sinister to try to save the planet? Maybe Professor Holden thought this way as well. What is the point of living if there is no planet to live on?

What would Earth look like in another twenty years? How bad will the natural disasters be over time? Are we as a society even making a dent in using renewable resources to offset the fossil fuels? What happens when we cut down all the trees?

My mind was spiraling with questions about humanity's future.

I didn't sleep at all, tossing and turning all night with questions I could not answer. I was trying to make peace with the computer's predetermined outcome as I battled through a sleep-deprived haze.

Could I really do this?

I spent most of Sunday morning in a zombified state as I ate my breakfast. I couldn't shake the thoughts out of my head as I stared into my bowl of cereal, stirring the milk in a circular motion.

Mom banged away in the kitchen cleaning her morning mess, obviously trying to get my attention while humming a song playing on the radio. Our kitchen is quite small but with newly updated cupboards, counters, floors and appliances. It was the only room in the house that looked new, which in itself would probably make a prominent feature in a magazine or something. The rest of the house looked like it creeped right out of the 1980s. Mom jokes that I have a lot of renovating to do and asks when I will be starting. I ignore it, of course.

"What's wrong with you this morning?" she asked.

"Oh nothing, couldn't sleep last night, that's all." I could never be truthful to her with what was really on my mind.

"You would tell me if something were really bothering you, wouldn't you?" she asked as she threw a dish towel over her shoulder.

"Yep, I would," I said, forcing a smile. I hated lying to my mother.

She stared at me for what seemed like ten minutes. Mothers always seem to know when something is wrong.

"OK. Well, I am here when you are ready to talk," she said, trying to be chipper.

As my mind was beginning to free itself

from the depressing thoughts, a news brief broadcast over the radio.

"Scientists are now predicting the polar ice caps are melting thirty times faster than previously thought. It is now believed they will be fully melted by 2080, twenty years earlier than previous assessments. Coastal cities are now faced with a heightened timeline for preparation!"

All the thoughts came rushing back with a heavy burden. I could do two things: speak into that microphone and use my voice to fix the world, or flip an electrical breaker and forget everything about this computer.

It wasn't a simple decision, given the heavy consequences.

* * * *

Mom left for work right on time, as usual for a Monday morning. I decided to skip work and call in sick. I made sure to steer clear of Mom in the morning, aware that she wouldn't buy my excuse if she saw me acting fine.

I acted as if I wasn't feeling well when speaking to my manager. He bought into the ruse and he himself suggested I stay home for a few days if I needed to. I couldn't help thinking this could be the last time I spoke to him.

The computer had explained it needed a landline phone. I wasn't even quite sure if they were still around. Everything is wireless these days.

Although this was extremely uncommon in today's world, I was able to have the phone company install a new line at the house.

This would be a special order, the phone company said, which probably meant they would try to talk me out of it. My persistence was worth it and I won the battle; they even came out THAT day to install the line, what service! I guess the technician already being in the neighborhood was to my advantage.

It was a simple procedure, really. He ran a phone cable from the cracking sun-beaten telephone pole to a gray weathered phone box located outside the house in record time.

The telephone man asked several times, "What do you need one of these for? I couldn't tell you the last time I installed one of these!"

"It may be old, but they are reliable?" I relayed a half answer, half question. It was the only answer I could muster without sounding like a complete goof.

Before he left, he helped to locate what the phone company called a termination block in my basement. I suspected that this wiring might lead straight into the bomb shelter; I hoped anyway, so I lied and told the telephone man it went to Mom's attic office.

* * * *

I slipped down into the bomb shelter for the second time after the telephone man drove off. The room was still eerie and loud as before, hot too.

The machine had the last question still printed on the screen with the lower blinking green line waiting for input.

I pressed the talk button on the microphone, thinking it would wake the machine from its slumber. "Hello."

"Hello Darren, would you like to replay the last calculated scenario?" asked the computer while its fans buzzed away.

"No." I said.

"Computer, what is the likelihood I will survive if we," I paused, "execute this plan?"

"If we gather an ample amount of supplies, the survival rate will be 100%. The recommended amount of food supplies is one to two years' worth."

A sudden realization hit me while I was at the terminal. I'm not prepared for anything, no supplies, no nothing!

* * * *

I abandoned the bunker and made the choice to follow the computer's suggestion. I grabbed Mom's credit card from the thick brown books, which she kept on her nightstand for emergencies.

Under normal circumstances, she would kill me for stealing this. There would not be any normal punishment or repercussions for using her credit card without permission, only a solid prison sentence. She would forbid me from leaving the house until my 18th birthday, for sure. I would be a prisoner for years, paying off my debt.

She'll thank me later. I tried to brush off the thought.

The grocery store was just a short bus ride down the road. I knew I could walk everything I needed back and forth to home. So, I was prepared to rack up thousands of dollars, buying food and supplies to store in the bomb shelter.

I was dead set on going through with this now, no turning back. I was determined to make sure that Mom and I would be set for several years, especially if we needed to spend a long amount of time in the bomb shelter.

I purchased as much non-perishable food as I could. Anything I saw that was dry food, I grabbed: canned vegetables, pasta, soup, fruit and meats all made it into my cart. I included bags of rice, beans, dried instant potatoes, salt and pepper, dried herbs, and a lot of bottled water. By the second trip of painstakingly carrying grocery bags back to the house, I was praying for my own car.

I also found myself at an outdoor recreational store further down the road, purchasing everything I could think of; batteries, camping gear, spare gas cans and a water purification system. This caused quite a few more back-and-forth trips to the house.

The checkout attendant gave me the weirdest look and asked what I was planning. I responded with the first thought on my mind, "Hey," I said chuckling, "haven't you ever met a doomsday prepper?"

I maxed out Mom's credit card, completely maxed it out. Each time I used it, I held my breath, hoping the checkout attendants wouldn't ask for identification, otherwise it would have been game over.

My mind stayed busy with thousands of 'what if' thoughts cycling through a sequence in my brain. I decided I would wait until Mom came home from work before I executed the computer's motive. Then, I knew she would be safe and we could rush into the shelter if any disaster struck close.

Throughout the afternoon, I brought down all the food and supplies into the shelter, placing them in any free space available. There was no room, so I began stacking the supplies on top of the mainframe and cramming what I could next to the desk. Living conditions might be cramped, but we would manage.

I filled the dozen gas cans I had purchased earlier at the filling station and filled each one to the brim, managing to do so on three trips alone. Down in the bunker, I filled the generator's gas tank, and I investigated how to start the thing, splashing the smelly gas on my hands.

I found the starter cord and pulled back on it three times. On the fourth pull, the engine seemed to slurp the gasoline into its cavity and rumble to life.

I let the engine run for a while and replaced the filter on the shelter's clunky carbon dioxide purification system by cutting out a piece of foam the exact size needed. It wasn't perfect, but I figured it should work. I flipped the switch to the system. It choked and barked until it maintained a steady hum.

Preparation is complete!

* * * *

I waited.

It was almost game time. I couldn't keep a single straight thought in line. I was bouncing between thoughts of the computer, what would happen around the city, the house, work, and everything else. I paced back and forth, practically making tread marks on the carpet.

Mom arrived home right on time, ready for her afternoon workout, as she usually does right after work.

I gave her a peck on the cheek and mentioned that I'll be occupied in the bomb shelter until dinner. "Go to your hole," she said. "Boys will be boys," she muttered.

Down in the bunker, I pressed the spacebar to free up the screen and waited patiently for the green blinking line.

"Welcome back Darren."

My voice quivered as I held down the green talk button. "Hello computer."

"Have you been able to obtain a landline telephone connection?" asked the computer.

"Yes." I said while holding the talk button.

Suddenly, a weird ringing noise in several pitches could be heard behind me. Something I wasn't quite used to hearing before, the dial-up modem.

"A dial-up connection test has been established. Thank you for restoring communications. Darren, would you like to replay the last calculated scenario?" asked the computer.

I looked behind me, half expecting Mom standing there, "Yes, yes, please run through the last scenario."

All fans on the mainframe instantaneously turned on at the same moment, the circle tape drives all spun at once. The screen displayed names and addresses of nuclear power plants stored in its database and scrolled through the list faster than I could effectively read.

"Cycling through the list of 200 stored

nuclear facilities. I will attempt to establish a connection with last known data and report facilities for final approval," said the computer.

The list of facilities started in the United States, and the computer slowly worked through the list. For each facility, the computer activated its dial-up modem and tested its connection, before disconnecting and moving onto the next list. The computer continued to facilities outside of the United States; France, Germany, and Japan.

The computer took close to a half an hour of testing and gathering data. I sat and watched its list scroll down on the screen. If the computer established a connection, it marked the last line with CONNECTED.

In the last thirty years, a lot has changed, and it astonishes me that some of these facilities are still connected to this outdated dial-up communication.

The room suddenly got quiet as the last facility on the list was marked as

CONNECTED. "I have completed the list," said the computer as the screen cleared all the text and a new list was presented on the screen. "I have discovered 29 facilities whom I am able to communicate with and still have the ability to initiate the plan. These facilities are also the oldest, with most residing in the United States and France. Based on my calculations, a meltdown at these facilities would be enough to trigger adequate chaos in society to effectively achieve the desired results. Would you like to execute?" asked the computer.

I paused and stared at the screen. Would I like to execute this plan? Would I? I could feel my heartbeat pounding in my throat.

"Please provide voice verification or type YES into the terminal."

I looked behind me, stalling my decision.

"Please provide voice verification or type YES into the terminal," the computer repeated.

I pressed the green talk button on the microphone, hopefully for the last time.

"Yes."

* * * *

I was shaking uncontrollably, climbing up the ladder. In order to save the planet, I had just become the world's biggest mass murderer. And no one would know my name, thank god.

My knee sank into the dirt as I advanced to the top and into the yard. I looked up in all directions, expecting something, anything.

But, I reached the top to find no change. Not even a tremble from an explosion that I was expecting. With the sun beginning to set, its fading red-orange light illuminated the back of our house.

I circled around in all directions up towards the sky, no change, nothing.

I could see Mom through the window, running on her treadmill, looking fatigued. A flock of sparrows fluttered overhead. I didn't understand.

Out of the corner of my eye, Robert rounded the corner to my backyard, smiling. He was still wearing his sweaty, dirt stained clothing from a hard day's work.

"Did anything happen?" I questioned frantically.

"What do you mean, did anything happen?" asked Robert, walking closer. "What are you talking about? What's wrong?"

"Nothing," I replied, feeling less tense. Perhaps the incidents haven't happened yet.

"I got a little information about the previous owner. Apparently, my wife is a friend of a friend of the professor's late wife and she talked quite a bit about their life."

"Oh really? Do you mind telling me a bit later? I'll stop by and get the details," I said, trying to divert a long conversation.

"Just a second Darren. The professor, named Javier, was a Psychology and Computer Science Professor at the university in town. The guy was a genius apparently and a real wizard with computers. That is how my wife put it: a wizard! He used technology to study the human response to intense situations and was working on some 10-year research study."

"Thanks for letting me know, Robert, but I need to get back to work here." I said, trying to get rid of Robert.

"Real quick, just one more thing. According to my wife, this guy became too intense with his research and the university fired him. He brought his research home with him to keep it going. Instead, he ended up being paralyzed when he was in a car accident and he spent the last several years of his life bedridden," explained Robert.

"Wait, you said he brought his research home with him?"

Something didn't feel quite right.

"Yea, I was thinking maybe he did some of that research down there in that shelter?"

It had been almost twenty minutes since the computer executed its plan and something wasn't right. I pulled out my cell phone and checked the news. There was nothing new beyond the normal news cycles. A large catastrophe would certainly hit the news airwaves instantly.

"Everything alright Darren? What did you find down there?"

Without responding to Robert, I turned and climbed down the bomb shelter shaft. Robert's voice trailed in the distance as I descended down the latter.

My foot slipped close to the bottom, and I ended up sliding to the base of the ladder, landing on my left foot. I grumbled as I turned towards the metal entrance, fighting through the pain of my newly twisted ankle.

I limped to the terminal to find nothing but a black screen. I pounded on the keyboard to wake the machine. Nothing.

The mainframe suddenly roared behind me with a momentary fan burst. For what felt like several minutes, the tape drives spun.

Simultaneously, the mainframe's indicator lights, green and red, all turned on. The green line on the terminal started listing letters at an excruciatingly slow rate.

I stood still as each letter printed on the screen and the glow of green text flashed on my face. It finally stopped, with a question filling the screen.

WOULD YOU LIKE TO PLAY AGAIN? (YES/NO).

ABOUT THE AUTHOR

Drew is a technology nut from Indiana who works in Information Technology writing software. When he's not writing code, he's writing words. He has written numerous flash fiction, short stories, and comic books. He founded the comic publishing company, SnowyWorks. More info can be found at https://snowyworks.com.

https://snowyworks.com